Coming From The Space

Crystal's Story

Allate Felicite Yavo

ISBN: 9798869015471

Dedication

To my family, specially to my children (Karen, Jonathan, and Kaitlyn), and to my friends who support me from the beginning of the writing of the book.

Acknowledgment

This book is a sci-fi book based on a real story. My thanks go to Divine Ghost Writers, who helped me in the writing process of the book. I thank my family, brothers, and sisters who encourage me to write this book, to my children, specially Karen Lilia Lawson, she is an amazing girl, but I have not forgotten, Jonathan and Kaitlyn. Those children are my gems. Thanks also to my friends and Everyone who help and support me.

CONTENTS

About the Author

The author Allate Felicite Yavo born in April 1979, is married and a mother of 3 children, professionally she is a businesswoman, and intellectually she has a master's degree in finance and is currently doing a Ph.D. in Public Policy and Administration at a university in the United States. Since her childhood, she has been passionate about reading books. She has compassion for people suffering and is very determined to achieve her goals.

Chapter 1

Orion, the capital planet of the galactic empire, seemed lonely from afar. An odd yet glazing cylinder approached the ground in silence. Its active sensors beeped loudly as they scanned the area for any danger.

Crystal sighed in exhaustion at the sight of her home. Just as her presence was detected, the planet came to life. The glazing cylinder let out a loud hiss, and a door nearby opened.

Crystal walked through the door and into the familiar building. She crossed one hallway as each door opened on its own. Finally, she entered a large facility where her Father and twin brother awaited.

"It's good to see you back, Crystal!" Crystal's Father beamed at her.

Crystal lowered her head in respect and replied, "It's good to see you too, Father."

"Were you able to finish your duty?" Crystal's Father immediately asked, as he knew other people awaited the good news.

"Yes, Father. It was not difficult. Even the people of the colony were tired of the tyranny. So, I did what I had to do to maintain peace in space. That's what you taught me."

"Great! I'm proud of you."

Crystal smiled. Never did she get tired of those words. They sounded like music.

"Now, you must get some rest." Harlan, Crystal's twin brother, urged with concern.

Crystal nodded in agreement. A wave of exhaustion took over her as she began to think back on all that had happened on her mission.

A tyrannical empire began to attack colonies throughout the known galaxy and forcibly absorbed a few of them into its territory. Crystal was originally sent to sort the problem through table talk. However, the emperor had gotten arrogant. Even the people of his colony had grown tired of him.

Thus, it didn't take long for Crystal to help overthrow the government. The arrogant emperor resisted and lost his life doing so. Soon after that, Crystal appointed a better leader for the colony and offered aid to help cover up the damages.

As Crystal walked toward her room, she passed a few people who bowed down to her. She smiled back at them in return. Most of them had witnessed her grow up. They had cared for her in ways no other colony does. People in most colonies feared their emperors. While Crystal, being a goddess, didn't prefer that treatment. Thus, she maintained such a close environment in the capital planet of the universe.

Crystal had still not gotten used to people bowing down to her. She felt like she never would. She began wondering about Inorth, the emperor she had just destroyed. She couldn't understand how he could be filled with so much arrogance in such a short amount of time. He was only able to establish his power over two colonies, and yet, his attitude seemed like he owned the world. On top of that, he was bold enough to dismiss Crystal, someone who did own the world.

Crystal walked into her room. Adria, Thelea, and Meruta stood up in alarm and bowed down. Once Crystal acknowledged their presence, they hurried forward and got busy with work.

They quickly but swiftly took off the armor suit and sat Crystal down in front of a wide mirror. A chill ran down her spine as the girls quickly put her in a silk gown. Crystal let herself feel the soft fabric against her skin. She hadn't realized how much she had looked forward to this moment. The days on her mission would have never allowed her to wear something of such sort. She had to be in the armor suit at all times for her safety.

Once she was sure she didn't need anything else, Crystal nodded at the girls, allowing them to leave her alone. She walked to the huge bed and sat herself down. Just as her head hit the soft pillow, she fell into a deep sleep.

Crystal woke up the next day more refreshed than ever. She allowed herself to walk in the garden alone for a while before going to her Father's chamber. She softly knocked on the door and let herself in.

"Ah, Crystal. Come in" Crystal's Father motioned her to sit down.

Crystal sat herself down and began to analyze the emotions on her Father's face. Judging from the lines on his forehead, it seemed like bad news was coming.

"You've grown up so fast, Crystal. I still remember when you were little and ran through these disturbing the peace of everyone in sight" Crystal's Father displayed a small smile.

"What's the matter, Father?" Crystal asked, concern lacing her tone.

"Nothing. I have just come to the realization that you no longer need us for every little problem. Instead, you are the solution to all the problems in this universe. And soon enough, I would have to give you away."

"What do you mean? I'm not going anywhere."

"Yes, you have to." Crystal's Father paused before finally speaking, "Remember what I taught you, Crystal. You need to always put others' needs before yours. It is your responsibility as a Goddess."

"Yes, Father. I remember it very well." Crystal assured with a smile, but her Father only looked at her with concern.

Crystal felt uneasiness settle in. She could sense her Father wasn't happy, so she moved closer and asked,

"Tell me, Father. What's wrong?"

"You are soon required to leave for another mission." Crystal's Father choked out the words.

"But, what's troubling you, Father? I go on missions all the time." Crystal was confused.

"It's not an easy mission, Crystal. And I know you will have to suffer a lot for it" Crystal's Father seemed like he was about to cry.

"It's okay, Father. It is my responsibility to ensure the universe is safe. I will try my best to make you proud." Crystal reassured her Father.

"I know you will, Crystal. I know you will." Crystal's Father smiled. "But you know I can never see you in pain. Which is why I think you should get married."

Crystal kept thinking back on her Father's words. She had never seen him worry like this, which meant the mission was going to be ten times more difficult than the last. However, marriage was something Crystal had never given much thought to. Throughout her childhood, she focused on her powers to test what she could do.

Crystal stopped in front of Harlan's chamber. She lightly knocked on the door and went inside.

"Did you know about the mission on Earth?" Crystal asked almost immediately.

"Father told you?" Harlan asked back.

Crystal nodded in reply, earning an exhausted sigh from Harlan. She plopped down on his bed and stared at him expectantly.

"We are all worried about you. The Earth is a cruel place to be. If anyone found out about you, they would do anything to sleep with you."

Crystal thought back on Harlan's words. She knew Harlan was right.

"This is why I asked Father to be with you in your journey. To support you and be there for you every step of the way." Harlan spoke with determination.

A million questions flooded her mind, but she resorted to the one she knew her brother would know the answer to.

"How do you know all of this?"

"I have my resources. Just like you do," Harlan gave a smug smile.

Crystal couldn't help but smile. She shook her head at her brother's remark.

"Hey. Stop worrying too much" Harlan gave a reassuring smile and placed his hand on Crystal's

"I'm not worried," Crystal assured. "I'm worried that Father is worried."

"He won't be. He knows I will take care of you." Harlan squeezed Crystal's hands for comfort.

Crystal was overwhelmed with emotions. She hugged her brother tightly.

"Dad was right," Crystal's voice was muffled in his shoulder. "We have grown up very fast."

That night, Crystal thought back on her life. She felt like her life was about to change. She knew more responsibilities would be on her lap. However, not for one moment did she doubt her own abilities. Also, she was smart enough to understand that with a God on her side, she could tackle any problem thrown her way.

A month later, Crystal got married to Harlan. A huge crowd cheered for them as Harlan placed a ring on Crystal's finger. She looked around and met the gaze of some of the people she had grown up with. They all fought back the tears as they saw their lovely Goddess being united with a God.

Chapter 2

The King of the Earth had suddenly gotten extremely ill. In the span of a few days, the youthful glow on his face had waned and withered as a plague festered on his cheeks and boils appeared on his body. In his dire condition, he needed help. If he didn't have a solution to his surmounting problems, the Earth would forever be separate from the other planets in the universe, and the tumultuous Red Sea would be perpetually barred from the land. It wasn't just the King who suffered. With each passing day, the people of Earth decayed and festered sickness. They lacked food and sleep and were in the clutches of eternal poverty. Even the ones among them who seemed to be rich had many kinds of problems.

Brimming with desperation, the King of the Earth started scouring the universe for any help that he might get. No matter how hard they pleaded and tried, no help would come. One day, however, one of his messengers informed him of Crystal and the monumental power that she wielded. Before the King could get his hopes up, the messenger informed him that there was a catch.

"While Crystal may be the only deity who can help us, she cannot leave her husband's side without his permission. We must appeal to the Great Harlan and ask him to allow his wife to come to Earth and help us,"

After listening to the messenger's words intently, the King decided to make a council that would convene and decide how to have Crystal's aid. The council consisted of people from all walks of life— pastors, mediums, Muslims— who all eagerly tried to see how Crystal could help them.

On the council's second day, an old, frail-looking woman wrapped in a flimsy shawl came up to the council and told everyone that she knew Crystal very well.

"I know all there is to know about Crystal and her twin brother, Harlan." The old woman said, her voice earnest.

"You may continue," The council urged her on.

"Crystal and her twin brother appeared in an egg in the universe to their Father, the almighty king of Venus. Just like her brother, she was born with multiple powers and prowess. When the twins came of age, they took each other as husband and wife."

"Oh, wise old woman," A pastor nodded his head enthusiastically and inquired. "How do we receive Crystal's aid?"

"The only way to get Crystal is to enter the spiritual world because Crystal came to our realms destined to be the Queen of the Universe. Her husband, Harlan, is only there to guide her, protect her, give her advice, decide for her, and love her."

After a small pause, the old woman let out a sigh and continued:

"Be warned, people of the Earth. Harlan is the only one who can decide if she can help the Earth because this mission is dangerous. I have been blessed with the gift of foresight, so I can see what most of you cannot. Crystal's future on Earth is not bright. She has to marry a man on this Earth who is responsible for all our suffering and defeat him without using her powers. Her powers may only be utilized when she is in great danger. Harlan is in no easy position either: does either of you know a man who would let his wife sleep with another man?"

"No, we do not," The council answered.

The old woman shook her head in dismay.

"Mark my words: Crystal will suffer here. Many people—men and women from all over the world, hailing from different walks of life-- will make their children sleep with her to have power and money. She will suffer here tremendously, falling into a sickness that will last for many long years. She will be poor, eating the crumbs of humility for all her time here, and in the eyes of everyone, she will be no better than a beggar."

"Is there no other way, wise woman?" A council member asked.

"No, there isn't," The woman answered. "Crystal has to know what poverty means to be able to help. But after that, the Earth will be free of any problems. But this is no cause for celebration.

The people of the Earth need to be warmed. If anyone harms her, they will have to face the wrath of Harlan."

After hearing the old woman's words, the King of Earth contemplated for a moment before speaking, "We will assure her protection on this Earth and give her everything she might need, and we won't let her go in deep suffering; we will always be there for her. But what should we do, old woman?"

The old woman said, "Enter the spiritual world and shout her name for many days and nights. The only one who can allow her to leave is her husband, and remember: it will be a difficult decision for Harlan because nothing like that has happened before."

The woman paused for a moment before continuing, as her eyes turned glazed.

"Beelzebub is this man on Earth that she will marry, and he is a spirit— a cruel one, at that, and he will make her suffer, knowing that she won't use her powers against him. But the time will come when she will make him bow down by spreading love all around the world. Love is Crystal's secret weapon. It is also her doom because it is her great heart that calls her to Earth's mission."

"Who are you, and how do you know all of this?" The King asked, baffled.

The old woman smiled and lowered her hood, which had been covering half of her face.

"The reason why I can do anything for Crystal—whose arrival on Earth will be a great honor for me is because I am the Earth Goddess."

Upon hearing these words, the council bowed down to her, saying, "Oh, great one, we are in honor of your presence between us, simple mortals."

The Goddess of the Earth retorted, "It is Crystal who deserved your honor. We will follow her everywhere, especially me. All the gods, goddesses, and spirits will help her. Yahweh, Lucifer, spirits and even Zeus will be helping her. We will let her decide everything on Earth, and she will have a secret identity, and we shall take care of her. I want to remind you that she talks to animals as a great Goddess. She gives birth to everything and is the beginning and the end; completely sufficient unto herself, and yet for us, she must suffer!"

The room filled with silence as the King of the Earth asked the Earth Goddess, "But won't she have children on this Earth?"

"She will have Harlan's children and Harlan's children only. We won't let anyone impregnate her, not even Beelzebub. It is to be understood by everyone that the marriage between Beelzebub and her will be fake, and he won't have any authority over her. "

"So be it!" The council members exclaimed.

Suddenly, the people on Earth heard a powerful voice in the universe saying:

"We heard all that you said, Earth's Goddess. We all heard you. The sound of your pleas ascended to the heavens, and I, Harlan, will decide tomorrow on a conciliatory with all the universe. Tomorrow, we will decide, but be careful. Crystal won't be able to use her powers on Earth, but if something happens to her, I will unleash my fury on you. I will erase the Earth and make it disappear. I hope you heard me. All the universe bows down before Harlan. You Earthlings are no different!"

Chapter 3

Eros, the God of Orion's galactic empire, paced back and forth in his chamber. He had been unable to decide on how to make Crystal appear on Earth without revealing her true self. Eros had never felt more nervous. He needed this mission to go perfectly. If not, who knows what the people of the Earth might do to Crystal?

Harlan was called into Eros's chamber. He knew his Father was worried and needed him there. He walked into his chamber and watched him pace back and forth.

"Father, I have come up with the solution for it," Harlan said, determination lacing his voice.

Eros stopped in his tracks and gazed at Harlan expectantly,

"What is it?"

"Crystal shall appear on Earth as a baby. She will be found in a cornfield by this man, Olian." Harlan showed him a picture of Olian.

"In Olian's custody, Crystal will be safe. She will grow up and get to experience the world fully." Harlan continued to explain. "This man has been crying and shouting the name of Crystal every day to come and help him."

"Who is this man?"

"He used to be a politician and just retired a few years ago. He spent most of his life running from one country to the other. But now he is settled into the place he came from." Harlan explained with pictures of Olian.

When Eros kept quiet, Harlan decided to continue,

"He needs Crystal, and Crystal needs him. People on Earth are going to make her suffer for being the daughter of a politician."

"What about you?" Eros asked, "I need you close to her when that happens."

"Yes, I considered that as well. I believe I would either take the form of a kitten or a puppy. Surely, Olian's family couldn't refuse such a creature from entering their home."

"That's a good plan." Eros nodded, "Explain everything to Crystal and prepare her for the mission. You need to leave the next morning."

Harlan nodded in reply and left the room.

***

When Olian woke up the next morning, he noticed the sky looked brighter than usual, even when the sun hid behind a grey blanket of low clouds. Olian couldn't help but stare at the sky with longing. Moments later, he heard a phone ring which snapped him back to reality.

He watched the phone ring in silence. When it finally stopped ringing, Olian went closer and turned it off. He then went downstairs, straight outside, and sat in his car.

Nebo, his long-known driver, got into the car and started it. Without even asking, Nebo took Olian where he had been going for the last few weeks. Olian sat back comfortably in his car and looked out onto the passing road. The car moved from a commercial area to an empty one. Huge green lands were soon in sight. The car halted at one of the corn fields.

Olian got out of the car and let the cool winds slap his face. He closed his eyes and let him breathe freely. The fresh smell of the corn leaves cleaned out his lungs.

Smiling to himself, he walked forward, pushing one of the tall leaves out of his way. A shiver ran down his spine as his feet touched the wet ground. He looked back on the road and saw his Nebo looking back at him with a bewildered expression.

"I'll be back!" Olian announced.

Nebo nodded, taking this as a sign to give him his space. He got into his car and did what he had done most of his life. He waited.

Olian had never dared to walk into the cornfield. Even as a child, he would run away when his Father insisted that he do so. Now, he couldn't believe he was willingly walking into it. As he was doing that, he realized there wasn't anything to be afraid of. He couldn't understand what frightened him at the sight of corn fields as a child.

Olian's pace had now increased. He walked as if he knew it very well. He took turns as if he knew the way out. Olian wouldn't have stopped if he hadn't heard the sound. At first, he didn't understand it among the voices of the leaves slapping each other. And then, he heard it again. It was the sound of a baby crying.

Olian found himself moving closer to the voice. He pushed away the leaves aggressively until he finally came across the small human responsible for the sound. He looked around and was dumbfounded by it.

'Why would anyone leave a baby here?' Olian thought to himself. 'The cruel world'

Olian took the baby in his arms, and like magic, she stopped crying. Instead, she looked at Olian and let out a tiny giggle. Olian found himself smiling back. He brought the baby's face closer to his chest. He then turned to walk and follow the steps he came in.

Once outside the cornfield, Olian noticed the baby had gone to sleep as it tightly clutched his shirt. He told Nebo what had happened and safely brought the baby back to his house.

As Olian held onto the baby on the drive back, he was taken back to the time he was in the hospital not long ago. The time when he was given the tragic news. That moment was still fresh in Olian's mind when his newborn was taken away from him. He remembered the horrid look on his wife's face. That was the moment when Olian realized there was nothing on Earth he could do to save the baby. He couldn't pull any strings this time; he wasn't God. Just a hated politician.

Olian went straight into his wife's bedroom when he got home. He thought she would cheer up at the sight of a baby. Perhaps, she would finally display her real smile.

Ever since their baby died, his wife had been lifeless. Although she kept a great façade in front of the kids, Olian knew the sadness her eyes held.

"Look whom I brought!" Olian displayed all the enthusiasm he could muster.

Effa, Olian's third wife, gasped. "What is that?"

"That's a very pretty baby girl" Olian smiled as he laid down the baby on her bed.

"Whose is it?" Effa asked with a sad smile. "She is beautiful."

"It's ours." Olian looked at Effa, who looked back at him with disbelief.

"What do you mean?"

Olian explained all that had happened at the cornfield while Effa was horrified,

“Who would leave a baby like that?”

“That’s what I want to know. But I made Nebo ask around, and no one seems to know.”

Effa looked at the baby with a sad smile. Not long ago, she was holding her own baby. But then, it was taken away from her in the next moment.

Effa blinked the memory away and dared to hold the baby in front of her. She gently picked her up and brought it closer to her chest. Her breath hitched as the scent of the baby traveled up her nose. She was beautiful. Effa didn’t realize when tears swelled up in her eyes. All she knew what that the baby was hers.

Chapter 4

"I have to go now," Harlan informed his dad, "Olian has founded Crystal. I've been following them, and now she is safe."

"What will I do now without you by my side?" Eros smiled sadly.

"I'll visit and be in touch," Harlan assured.

"Please take care of Crystal." Eros sounded his worry.

"No worries, Dad. I have to go now. This woman needs to find me as a kitten."

Back on Earth, large pillows of dark clouds were gathering. A loud thunder echoed as if warning the people of Earth about Harlan's entrance. Effa ordered the servants to close all the windows. She didn't want the cool winds to make Crystal sick.

The sky began to thunder more ferociously. Soon, it began to drizzle, and puddles began to form. A few more claps of thunder later, the rain became more intense.

Effa decided to check up on Crystal; sure enough, the baby was awake from the pitter-patter of the rain on the ceiling. From the looks of it, Crystal seemed uneasy since she couldn't settle in the comfortable crib. At the sight of Effa, the baby began to wail.

Effa brought Crystal closer to her chest and took her to the living room, where Olian seemed distracted by the television. Sitting beside Olian, Effa rocked Crystal back and forth to put her back to sleep finally. She glanced at the television without realizing she was trapped in a trance.

"I think we should find a kitten for Crystal," Effa uttered, the only thought clouding her mind.

Olian looked back at Effa, who seemed lost in her own world. Before shifting his attention back to the television, he asked,

"Why do you say that?"

"Crystal needs a friend," Effa informed.

'How did you know Effa? It's like you are reading my mind.' Crystal thought to herself.

"I don't think so; she has her siblings, don't you think?" Olian sighed.

"She needs a kitten, Olian." Effa urged, her pitch higher than usual.

Olian looked at Effa with furrowed brows. He couldn't understand what had suddenly gotten into his wife.

"Are you okay?" Olian asked with worry lines on his forehead.

Effa had a strange look in her eyes. Her face had lost all color, and she was staring deep into Crystal's soul.

"Let me tell you a secret." Effa turned to Olian and whispered. "I am frightened, Olian. This baby is not what we think it is."

"What are you saying?" Olian couldn't understand a word that came out of his mouth.

"I discovered that this baby is Crystal, the almighty goddess," Effa whispered, her eyes bulging out of her sockets.

Just as the words came out of her mouth, Effa lost herself. The world began to spin, and soon her face made contact with the floor.

A while later, Effa woke up and saw Olian in the same state as her. He stirred as well and woke up just as surprised as Effa. Like a flood, memories came flashing through Olian's eyes. He remembered meeting a Chinese man who had told him all about the Goddess Crystal. He could now understand what Effa meant.

Before them stood Crystal, the almighty Goddess. For a moment, nobody moved. They couldn't understand what was happening. Once their minds finally registered to the situation, both bowed before the Goddess.

"Praise to the Goddess, the almighty, the Queen of creation. Praises from all that are alive and breathe." Effa found herself saying out loud.

Crystal nodded, acknowledging the praises before saying,

"You must be surprised to learn this about me, but it is all according to my plan. Last night, I appeared to the Chinese man who told me about you. He is going to be one of my masters on Earth."

"Surely, everything is your plan. You are all-knowing." Effa kept her gaze fixed on the floor.

"Now, Olian, you should go to a house and get a kitten for me. I will guide you but be careful; the right one is orange and white."

Olian dared to look back at the shining light coming from Crystal. His eyes were getting blinded by Crystal's true self, but he couldn't help it. He was dumbfounded about the task he was being given.

"No worries, you will recognize him because he is the only one with the color. Be careful again when you hold him because he is Harlan, my husband." Crystal assured Olian.

They bowed down before her again and left. Soon enough, Olian began his mission. He was still unsure how he was supposed to find the kitten, but he trusted God's process. After a long time, he felt a sense of contentment wash over him. He felt delighted to be able to be of some use to God.

Hours later, Olian stood in front of what seemed like an abandoned house. A small flickering light through the window told another story, though. He could see shadows moving across the home. Olian approached the house, entangling himself in cobwebs. He knew in his heart the kitten was inside.

Before he could go in, he had to make six rounds around the house and rig the entrance door as Crystal had instructed him to do so. Thankfully, cool winds began to blow slowly, making the rounds easier. Once he was done with the rounds and out of breath, he reached the front door and began to rig the door.

Nickie, the house owner, came to the front door, bothered by the loud noises. Just as Olian came in sight, she began to cry. She couldn't believe her eyes.

"Praise to the Lord! Praised to the Lord!" Nickie yelled, tears pouring down her face. "We need to pray, Olian."

"How do you know my name?" Olian asked with surprise.

"We need to pray, Olian. We want Harlan to manifest himself for protection and blessings." Nickie urged, trapped in a trance.

"Young woman, how do you know my name?" Olian insisted.

"I know you from the beginning of your political activities. I followed all the news about you, but I didn't know you were back in this country where you suffered a lot; you have been jailed so many times. How come it's here you choose to retire? I don't understand Mr. Olian."

"I made a deal with the power in place that I will stop all my political activities. I was told I would be killed if I tried my political activities again. I came with all my family, but my elder children are with their mothers. I am living alone here with Effa, my new wife." Olian responded

"What a small world, Mr. Olian. Never mind, you are welcome here. No need to explain to me the reason for your visit as I already know what it is for. This kitten you came for has spoken to me and explained everything to me, so you can have him." Nickie gave an assuring smile.

Olian began to reach for the kitten but was interrupted,

"Before that, we have to pray by calling our almighty goddess by her name."

Olian nodded with understanding, and both began to shout out the name of Crystal. She appeared to them with Harlan.

"I can't thank you enough for being so helpful in my mission." Crystal smiled, bringing warmth to the cold house.

"Thanks for gracing us with your presence," Nickie whispered, tears spilling from her face.

“My praises go to Harlan as well. Without his support, I couldn’t reach where I am now.” Crystal smiled at Harlan.

Harlan smiled back at Crystal before turning his attention to Olian,

“Our identities should be kept a secret. You should call me Minet.”

Olian nodded, keeping his gaze fixated on the ground. In a split second, Crystal disappeared while Harlan transformed into a kitten. Olian took Minet, wrapped him with a nice cover as Crystal instructed, and returned to his house.

When reaching his house, he put Minet, the cat, near baby Crystal. After that day, Minet the cat never left Crystal alone. Both comforted each other; before anyone knew it, they started growing together.

When Crystal turned five months old, Effa left her alone to shower. Harlan and Crystal took that opportunity to change into their true self. They made love as Effa showered in the next room. Once they were done, Crystal turned into a baby once again, while Harlan turned into a snake to keep her entertained. A while later, Effa checked in on Crystal and was shocked. Frightened, she ran away.

Years later, Effa got pregnant and gave birth to a baby girl. At that age, Harlan and Crystal were seven years old. Once in a while, Harlan would duplicate himself and appear as Uncle Urhan.

Once, Uncle Urhan was living in Olian's house because of a ceremony. He informed Olian that the ceremony was supposed to open Crystal's human eyes so she could see the spiritual world in her human body.

That night, Crystal entered Uncle Urlan's bedroom. Harlan took her to his bed and started kissing her. Olian and his wife Effa were in the corridor waiting for the spiritual awakening to happen and finish.

After Harlan kissed her, Crystal began to see the spiritual world as a human. She saw a rat with a human body and started screaming,

"Daddy! Daddy! What is that?"

Nobody could see what she was talking about. Her Father brought her closer to the window to distract her, but then Crystal saw a big fireball approaching her. She started screaming again,

"Daddy! Daddy! See the fireball?"

Olian couldn't see anything. He knew Crystal had to go through this to understand the world at a deeper level. He wished there was some way he could help his daughter. But once again, he was hopeless.

Chapter 5

A 6-year-old Crystal tossed and turned in her bed. She felt an uneasiness creep in, making it difficult to sleep. She couldn't understand what would finally get her back to sleep. She pushed the covers away from her body, tired of feeling hot one moment and then cold the next.

Crystal got up and hopped off of her bed. The house was dead silent. At this point, all the servants must've also gone to sleep. She cautiously took the stairs and entered the lounge area. No one was in sight, but she could hear faded sounds of conversation from a distance. She knew her dad was awake.

Crystal stopped for a moment to ponder on what to do. She knew Dad would be disappointed to see her still awake. In her defense, she had tried so hard to sleep, but her mind kept her awake.

Crystal inched closer to the study room. She peeked inside and could see her dad talking to someone on the phone animatedly. The door creaked loudly, grabbing her dad's attention, and he could finally see Crystal standing at the door.

Olian urged the person on the other line to finish the conversation,

"You know what? I'll call you later."

Once he heard the beep ringing in his ear, he called out to Crystal,

"Crystal! Come on in."

Crystal shyly moved closer and let the door close behind her.

"Why are you still up, sweety?" Olian asked gently.

"I couldn't sleep." Crystal pouted.

"Oh no. Why don't you try and sleep here on the couch while I do some work?" Olian suggested.

Crystal nodded and plopped on the couch in the corner. She rested her head on it, taking in the smell of leather.

"Dad? Can I ask you something?" Crystal finally decided to voice the thoughts she had been wondering about since morning.

"Yes?" Olian replied distractedly.

"Who are these women in the pictures?" Crystal asked innocently.

"What pictures?" Olian asked, still distracted by something.

"The pictures on your desks." Crystal reminded, grabbing Olian's attention

Olian took a pause to look at the pictures once again. There were a lot of them, but then, Olian had a big family. He had always wanted one. Too bad he couldn't keep them all together.

Olian's eyes landed on the picture in the far-end corner. The woman smiled back at him; the sparkle in her eye was blinding. Her brunette locks covered most of her smile, but it brought a smile to Olian's face for some reason. The picture was taken at their wedding.

Olian couldn't help but smile sadly at the picture. He had just gotten the worst news of his life and needed to be with his wife. He knew she needed him the most at this moment, but he couldn't do anything for her.

His oldest son, Mylam, had been a subject of his past life. Being a politician was never easy, and that's what Olian had told Mylam. However, he hadn't listened. He wanted to prove to the world what a good politician his Father was and how he could make amends for Olian's mistakes.

As usual, Olian's enemies got in the way and got Mylam murdered. Olian didn't understand what to do. He knew going to France would be dangerous for him and his family. He couldn't afford to lose anyone else. But the woman in the picture was calling out to him.

"This woman here," Olian picked up the picture frame, "is your stepmother."

"Stepmother?" Crystal asked, brimming with curiosity.

"Yes. I met her back then when I went to France. We were both students of agricultural engineering. She was one of the brightest students in class while I was just a loser." Olian laughed, "And then I married her. We had nine beautiful children."

"Wow. Where are they now?"

"Unfortunately, they had to stay back in France for their safety."

Crystal knitted her eyebrows in confusion. 'Safety?' She wanted to ask but kept quiet.

"And who's the other woman?"

"She's your stepmother too!" Olian replied with a smile.

"I'm going to take you to meet her one day. We have two children together, and I'm sure you'd get along with them." Olian explained.

"Cool," Crystal remarked in the same tone as her sister. She had heard her sister speak this way and had adopted the same style.

Crystal loved hanging out with her family. So much so that she had started dreading the time of sleep; she hated going to sleep. She just wanted to stay up late and play hide and seek with her siblings.

"Now, I know you don't want to go to bed, but it's very late, Crystal. You have to wake up early for school as well." Olian reasoned.

Crystal pouted at Olian, not accepting his reasoning at all.

"Come on, Crystal. Your brothers and sisters are sleeping too! What will you do all night?" Olian reminded.

Crystal looked around the room, finally acknowledging the silence in the house. She looked back at Olian, whose eyes were begging for her to sleep. She sighed in defeat and quietly headed back to her room. Sleep overtook her to the world of dreams just as her head hit the pillow.

Downstairs in the study, Olian wished for sleep to come. However, he knew no amount of sleeping pills would be able to work on him now. The news he had just received had knocked out the ground beneath him. He didn't know if he would be able to recover from that loss.

Finally, being enveloped by the silence, Olian let himself weep. Memories of his beloved son flashed before his eyes as his shoulder shook with each sob. How could he let that happen to his own blood and flesh?

Olian wished the ground to take him. He didn't want to live with guilt and shame. The phone rang once again, snapping Olian out of his grief. He let it ring for a while, taking deep breaths to console himself. He cleared the lump in his throat and picked up the phone,

"Hello?" The voice still came out weakly.

"Hello, Sir. This is Gabriel speaking." Olian's old bodyguard greeted. "We've been investigating the matter, and it seems like Sir Mylam had been poisoned."

Olian stifled a gasp. He didn't understand how it was possible. Mylam had been trained to avoid this from happening since there had been a number of poisoning attempts, not only on him but on all of Olian's children.

Somehow, he swallowed a sob and continued to speak,

"Who did this?"

"We're not yet sure about that, Sir. There are a few suspects, but they refuse to speak."

"Gabriel, you better find those sons of a bitches. Bring him to me. I'll show them what it feels like to cross Olian."

Olian slammed the phone on the table, a million thoughts crossing his mind. His body bubbled with anger as he threw the stack of files on the ground. He couldn't understand what to do. He was helpless.

In that state of misery, his eyes automatically landed on the picture of his wife. He gazed at it for a while, absorbing all the comfort he could get. His vision blurred, and Olian let the tears fall down.

Chapter 6

Seven-year-old Crystal sat on the floor of her room, surrounded by her favorite toys—a porcelain doll and a cuddly blue teddy bear. Her imagination transformed the room into a magical kingdom, where her doll was the Queen and the teddy bear her loyal protector. Crystal's parents, Olian and Effa, observed their daughter from the doorway, marveling at her ability to truly act like a child.

Effa smiled affectionately. “It's so fascinating to watch her, isn't it? She truly behaves like any other child her age.”

“I see that, Effa. I never doubted her ability to do so.” Olian grinned with pride.

The door creaked open, and Crystal’s parents walked inside.

“What’s our little doll up to today?” Olian asked in a sweet voice.

“Mama, Papa,” Crystal began, her voice brimming with enthusiasm, “I have so many stories to tell you! The Queen and the protector went on a daring adventure today, and they met new friends along the way.

Maria and David exchanged a glance. They were well aware of the imaginary world of Crystal. The doll was the Queen, and the teddy bear was the protector. They leaned in closer, eager to hear the tales Crystal had woven today.

Once Crystal was done telling her parents all about the fairyland, she surprised her Father with an unexpected question,

“Dad! Can I please attend school now? I’m 7 years old. All kids my age go to school. Why can’t I?”

Effa and Olian exchanged worried glances, unsure of how to proceed. Olian had always been protective of Crystal, as she was not an ordinary child. Her existence was a secret they had guarded carefully, afraid of the consequences if the truth were to be revealed.

Crystal’s eyes searched her Father's face for a response. Olian took a deep breath, considering the options before him. He knew that Crystal possessed incredible intelligence and a thirst for knowledge beyond her years. Denying her the opportunity to attend school would only stifle her potential and leave her feeling isolated.

‘This is not an easy decision. How will I protect you or keep your extraordinary abilities a secret?’ Olian thought to himself.

He knew going to school would mean exposing Crystal to the world.

Crystal could hear his Father’s thoughts but kept quiet. She had always sensed the fear and apprehension in her parents, but her curiosity about the world had grown stronger with time.

“Dad,” Crystal began, her voice filled with determination, “I promise to be careful. I won't reveal anything that could put us in danger. Please, give me a chance to learn, to make friends like other children."

Effa watched her daughter with a mixture of pride and worry. She understood Crystal's desire but couldn't help but fear for her safety. She placed a hand on Olian's arm, silently urging him to consider their daughter's plea.

Olian took a deep breath, his heart torn between protecting Crystal and nurturing her blossoming potential. After a moment of contemplation, he nodded, his resolve firm.

"Alright, Crystal," he said, his voice laced with both concern and encouragement. "I will enroll you in a school, but you must promise to be cautious. Your safety comes first, and we trust you to make the right decisions."

Crystal's face lit up with joy as she threw her arms around Olian. "Thank you, Dad! I won't let you down, I promise."

Over the following days, Olian and Effa diligently researched the best schools in the area, searching for one that would cater to Crystal's unique circumstances. They finally found a prestigious institution known for its emphasis on growth.

On Crystal's first day of school, Effa carefully prepared her for the new journey ahead. As Crystal entered the school gates, her heart raced with anticipation. She marveled at the buzzing atmosphere, the sound of children laughing, and the sight of classrooms filled with knowledge waiting to be discovered. She took a deep breath, reminding herself of the promise she made to her parents.

Crystal stepped into the classroom with a quiet demeanor. Mr. Michael, the teacher, welcomed her, introducing her to the class.

"We have a new student," he announced. "Her name is Crystal. Please show her everything we did before."

Excited chatter filled the room as all the children turned towards Crystal, their voices blending together as they greeted her in unison, "Good morning, Crystal!"

Crystal felt a mixture of nervousness and anticipation as she shyly waved her hand in response.

Rachel, Mr. Michel's daughter, approached Crystal with a friendly smile. "Come, Crystal, and sit with Donald," she said, leading her towards a vacant seat next to a boy named Donald, who was the son of another teacher.

Crystal quietly followed Rachel, taking her seat beside Donald. She greeted him with a soft "Hi," and Donald responded in kind.

As the days passed, Crystal continued her journey through primary school, attending classes and completing assignments diligently. She possessed knowledge beyond her years, but she purposefully behaved as if she was learning, not wanting to draw attention to her exceptional abilities.

During breaks, Crystal often found herself standing alone, observing her classmates as they played and interacted. She occasionally engaged in conversation with Rachel, finding comfort in her company. However, she remained cautious not to form deep connections that could potentially expose her true nature.

Crystal's only genuine interaction with the other children came during one playtime session when she joined them for a game. They laughed and played together, blissfully unaware of Crystal's hidden abilities. It was a rare moment of innocent joy that Crystal cherished.

Similarly, Crystal joined a group of classmates for a swim in a nearby stream. The cool water splashed against their skin as they laughed and splashed around. Crystal reveled in the experience, enjoying the camaraderie, but she made sure to keep her abilities hidden, blending in seamlessly with her peers.

Crystal's careful approach allowed her to navigate school life without drawing undue attention. She observed, learned, and adapted, but she never revealed her true potential.

In the days that followed, Crystal immersed herself in her studies, eager to absorb every bit of information she could. She excelled in every subject, quickly becoming a model student. The other children were drawn to her kindness and intellect, forming a circle of friends who admired her without knowing the true extent of her abilities.

Crystal remained true to her word, careful not to reveal her exceptional talents. She became known as an empathetic and brilliant girl, beloved by her peers and respected by her teachers. In this way, she successfully navigated through school, all while keeping her secret safe.

Even within the comfort of her home, Crystal maintained the facade of a normal child. She spent her days engrossed in playful activities, whether it was chasing after Minet, the family cat, or engaging in imaginative adventures with her little sister. Crystal's parents, Effa and Olian, treasured these moments, grateful for the semblance of normalcy they brought into their lives.

Crystal's meals mirrored those of any other child her age. She delighted in the sweetness of candies and cookies, savoring each bite with unadulterated joy. Effa lovingly prepared a variety of dishes for her daughter, ensuring she enjoyed a balanced diet of rice, bananas, fish, meat, and an assortment of vegetables and fruits. Among her favorites were pineapples, which happened to grow abundantly on a farm not far from their home.

One day, Olian took Crystal to one of the 500 acres of land. In the cool winds, Crystal found solace and a temporary escape from the weight of her hidden abilities. Sitting on the ground, she watched as her Father, Olian, tended to his tasks nearby. Unbeknownst to both of them, a slithering presence emerged from the underbrush—an ominous snake making its way toward Crystal.

Sensing the movement, Crystal turned her gaze and locked eyes with the serpent. In that instant, a flicker of recognition passed between them before the snake hastily retreated. It was Beelzebub, an ancient being who possessed a keen awareness of Crystal's true nature.

From that moment onward, Crystal's life took an unexpected turn. The realization of her extraordinary abilities became apparent to certain individuals, and whispers of her uniqueness spread throughout her school. Despite her efforts to blend in and maintain a sense of normalcy, Crystal found herself subjected to increasingly cruel treatment.

Instead of admiration or support, some students resorted to petty acts of jealousy. They began slipping coins into the covers of her assignments, mocking her achievements by turning them into symbols of disdain. It was a cruel reminder that Crystal's differences were not celebrated but instead used against her.

On one particularly unsettling day, an unknown individual took their harassment to a more personal level. With a daring intrusion, someone deposited an unidentified object in Crystal's hair.

Once Crystal reached home, Effa discovered the intrusion and swiftly washed Crystal's hair, her face a mask of concern. In the pits of her heart, she knew there was nothing she could do to stop them.

All these acts of malevolence were orchestrated by Beelzebub, who had uncovered Crystal's presence. The ancient being, envious of her extraordinary abilities, sought to expose and exploit her for his own gain.

Chapter 7

Mister Olian sat alone in his dimly lit living room, staring at the slab of meat on the table brought by one of his estranged brothers. He couldn't help but wonder why his brother had brought him this offering, especially considering the tense and strained relationship between them.

He glanced at the nervous smile on his brother's face and then fixed his attention back on the meat. Olian sat in silence, lost in thought, as he contemplated the meaning behind this unexpected gesture. Not a single word was uttered, but the tension between them was palpable. It was as if the air itself was holding its breath, waiting for someone to break the silence.

Effa decided she couldn't take it anymore. She rolled her eyes at her husband's rudeness and decided to fill the deathly silence with positivity.

"It is wonderful that you came. The kids were asking about you." Effa chirped, grinning ear to ear.

"They must be at school. I wouldn't want to intrude on their routine." Cielo, Olian's brother, chuckled nervously.

"Oh no, stop. They would love to meet you. You can stay as long as you want." Effa waved a hand in the air and proceeded to pick up the meat on the table. "Thanks for bringing this along!"

"You're welcome," Cielo gulped, his eyes focused on the meat that was now in Effa's hands.

"Stay until lunch, at least. I was just going to prepare it for Olian." Effa invited with a warm smile.

"Thanks, Effa, but please don't bother. My business awaits. I will leave as soon as I meet the kids." Cielo attempted to display a sad smile.

Olian sat there in silence as the uneasiness crept in, its burden increasing with each second. Soon enough, the kids arrived at the scene, brightening up the dull atmosphere of the living room.

They greeted their uncle and got busy listening to his adventurous stories about all the towns he had traveled to. While the kids listened to their uncle ramble on and on, Crystal's attention was focused on her Father. As she looked at Olian, who sat in silence, lost in thought, she knew it was time. It was obvious. The uneasiness evaporated from him and loomed over Crystal like a dark cloud.

She watched her Father, unable to digest the helplessness she felt. Despite being a goddess, there was nothing she could do to help. Despite the countless powers she possessed, she was helpless. She couldn't risk revealing her true abilities.

She slowly crawled toward her Father and placed her small hand on his. Up close, she could see her Father had accepted his face. His eyes had already lost their warmth and color. Crystal's heart broke as she squeezed his hand with all her might. Olian forced himself to smile, putting on a mask of bravery. For him, it was an honor to be of service to the Goddess.

On the other end, in the kitchen, Effa cooked the meat in silence. Effa stood over the sizzling pan, the aroma of the cooking meat filling the small kitchen. Once she knew it was cooked just the way Olian liked, she carefully placed it on the plate. She walked back to the living room and informed Olian that lunch was ready. A glance at Olian's and Effa knew something was wrong. Effa couldn't help but notice the sadness in his gaze.

"Would you like some vegetables with your meat?" she asked, trying to lighten the mood.

But Olian shook his head. "No, just the meat. I want to savor every bite."

Effa couldn't understand why he was being so dramatic. But as she watched him eat, she began to feel a sense of unease. Olian ate slowly, savoring each bite as if it were his last.

"Are you okay?" Effa asked finally, concern lacing her tone.

Olian nodded. "I'm fine."

As his gaze met Effa's, he realized his wife shouldn't be a witness to what was about to come.

"I'm going to take this upstairs, at the balcony. I want to enjoy this with an amazing view." Olian grinned.

Effa watched her husband in silence, pushing down the strange feeling in her chest. Olian stood up and grabbed the plate with a newfound enthusiasm. He gave his wife a peck on the cheek and left the living room, leaving her alone with the empty pan and the lingering scent of cooked meat.

Olian could already feel a tingling in his throat. His breathing had shortened, and his mouth suddenly became dry. The plate was now empty, and Olian felt thirsty. He opened his mouth to call out to his servant, but no sound came out. He tried once again but failed. Panic set in as he realized what had happened. It was as if the meat had cast a spell on him.

***

Olian had secluded himself in his home for three days straight. He didn't leave his house or even open the curtains to let in the sunlight. His friends and family were worried about him, but he seemed content to be alone with his thoughts.

On the fourth day, the family finally convinced him to seek professional help. Despite the best efforts of the medical staff, the day passed by in a blur of worry and fear. On the fifth day, the family was left heartbroken as their loved one slipped away from this world.

Whispers of Olian's death spread like wildfire. At first, rumors had started from an unknown source, but they quickly gained traction as people began to speculate on the cause of his demise. Some whispered of foul play, while others simply shook their heads in disbelief.

A few days later, they brought Olian's body to his house. The family was devastated as they brought him inside and laid him on his bed. They couldn't believe that their beloved Olian was gone forever. The sound of weeping filled the air, a mournful chorus that echoed off the walls. It was a scene of profound sadness, a moment when the weight of grief seemed almost too much to bear.

Effa sat on the edge of her bed, tears streaming down her face. She couldn't believe what had happened. Her heart felt heavy, and her mind was in a fog. She had lost something so precious to her. She couldn't imagine life without him. Yet, all she could do was cry and hope that somehow, someway, things would get better.

Crystal didn't know how to deal with the situation. She wondered if she should console her mother or put a bandage on her broken heart. All she knew was the fact that she was now alone in this world.

That night, she stood on Olian's balcony, expecting to feel his presence. She couldn't help but wonder what the future held for her. She had always known that life would be difficult, but she had never imagined it would be this hard. Would she be able to overcome the challenges that lay ahead, or would she be consumed by them?

She felt a deep sense of despair wash over her, as she knew this was only the beginning of her trials. Like Effa, she also had to hope everything would get better with time.

She looked up at the sky and saw a shooting star streaking across the darkness. Mesmerized by its beauty, she stood there for a moment, watching as it disappeared into the distance. She smiled to herself. It was all the reassurance she needed.

It reminded Crystal of the time Olian had taken her stargazing one night. Crystal closed her eyes and let out a deep breath. The memory of that day flooded her mind, as vivid as if it had happened just yesterday. They were both sitting under a mango tree, and Olian had shown Crystal a star in the sky.

"Never forget where you come from, Crystal," he had said, his voice low and steady. "That star up there, it's a reminder of your roots, of the journey that brought you here."

Crystal had listened intently, hanging on his every word. She had felt safe and happy in his presence, as if nothing in the world could harm her. She longed to go back to that day, to relive those moments with Olian. But she knew that was impossible. All she could do was hold onto the memory and treasure it forever.

Crystal gazed up at the twinkling night sky, her eyes fixated on a particular star that seemed to shine brighter than the rest. A sense of clarity washed over her. It was as if a puzzle piece had finally clicked into place, and she knew exactly what he was trying to say. All the gods of the universe had paid their homage to Olian. He was now, literally, in a better place.

That night, on multiple occasions, Crystal was woken up from her sleep. Her dreams were interrupted by a faint voice calling her name. She rubbed her eyes and listened closely, hearing it again - Olian's voice calling out to her. She hesitated for a moment, unsure if she should respond, but ultimately decided to ignore it and go back to sleep.

One day, Crystal saw Effa standing outside, cursing the power in place.

"You finally killed my husband, but if you are a stone, you won't die. If you are not one; you will die too!"

Crystal heard the words, feeling sad. She understood her frustration but felt anger for herself. She knew Effa would soon be able to meet Olian, leaving her all alone in this world. She wondered what she would do when Effa died too. She knew the bad news awaited her in the future.

Without Olian, Effa soon realized that it was impossible, with little income, to take care of all her children. Effa made the difficult decision to leave Crystal and her little sister home alone to look for a job. She knew that they would be safe and happy there. She took her little boy with her and desperately searched for someone who would help her even after knowing who her husband was. She knew that she would miss her daughters terribly, but she also knew that she had made the right decision for their future.

A year later, the news of Effa’s death also spread quickly. As the sun set over the small town, a somber mood hung in the air. It had been five years since her beloved husband had left this world, and now she had joined him in the great beyond. The townspeople gathered to pay their respects, sharing stories of the kind and generous woman she was.

As the night wore on, the stars twinkled above, a reminder that even in the darkest of times, there was always a glimmer of hope.

Chapter 8

Theresa was heartbroken after the sudden passing of her daughter, Effa. She knew she had to take care of Effa's children, and as per Effa's last wish, she took the children to her village. Effa had expressed the children needed to be sent to the village for their safety.

The journey was long and arduous, but Theresa was determined to give her grandchildren a better life. As they arrived in the village, the children were amazed by the lush greenery and the vibrant culture. The villagers welcomed them with open arms and were eager to help Theresa raise the children.

Despite the challenges they faced, Theresa was grateful for the opportunity to be with her grandchildren and to watch them grow up in a place filled with love and hope. Her pride and joy were her little ones, and she relished the opportunity to share their smiles and laughter with others.

As the night grew dark, Theresa led Crystal and her little sister to the bedroom where all the children in the house were sleeping. The room was dimly lit by a small lamp in the corner, casting eerie shadows on the walls. Crystal couldn't help but feel a sense of unease as she gazed at the sleeping figures of the other children.

The following day, Theresa came to wake up the children to sweep the compound together. That was the start of Crystal's real training. The next morning, Crystal woke up alone and swept the compound. When the other children woke up and saw what Crystal had done, they were so amazed and began to like Crystal.

A few days later, Theresa took her grandchildren for school admission.

“Hello, Mrs. Smith,” Mr. John said with a warm smile. “It's great to see you again. I'm happy to hear that you want your grandchildren to start school soon. We have some excellent programs here that I think they'll really enjoy.”

Theresa breathed a sigh of relief. She had been worried that the school might not have room for her grandchildren or that they couldn't afford the tuition. But Mr. John seemed genuinely interested in helping them. As they discussed the details, Mrs. Smith couldn't help but feel hope for her grandchildren's future.

“By tomorrow, let them start school. They are welcome here, Ms. Theresa, but we will evaluate them tomorrow and see in which stage they should go.” Mr. John explained with a small smile.

“Thank you so much, Mr. John.”

“You are more than welcome,” replied Mr. John.

The next day, the children stood nervously outside the school building, waiting for the test that would determine which classes they would be placed in. They fidgeted with their backpacks and whispered to each other, wondering what kind of questions would be on the test and if they had studied enough. The test was easy for Crystal, and she was done with it very soon.

Mr. John called his assistant and told him to immediately go to Ms. Theresa and tell her to come as quickly as possible. The test results were in his hands, and he was shocked. Once he found himself alone with Theresa, he spoke with urgency,

"Please, I need to know who Crystal is."

"Why do you want to know?" Theresa asked, her tone laced with worry. Effa had told her everything about Crystal.

"There is something strange with this child. She passed all the tests and even corrected her elders in 5th grade. She has to skip the 4th grade to be in 5th grade," said Mr. John.

'I am finished. If those villagers discovered who Crystal really is, it would be so terrible for all of us.' Theresa thought to herself.

"Thank you so much, Mr. John, but I preferred her to stay in 3rd grade because she is still a child." Theresa kept her tone confident.

Thankfully, John acknowledged it and said nothing else.

That night, Theresa retreated to her bedroom, her heart pounding with anticipation. She knew what she had to do. She closed her eyes and began calling Crystal out from the spiritual world. Suddenly, there she was - Queen Crystal, standing before her in all her glory. Theresa took a deep breath and spoke, her voice trembling with reverence.

"Your Highness, I am but a mortal human, yet I have been chosen to be one of your trainers on this Earth. If you would permit me, I would like to offer you some advice."

Crystal regarded her with a steady gaze, her expression unreadable. "Go ahead, Theresa."

"Please don't show your real potential to people. You have to fake sometimes as if you don't know anything. I will advise you to fail the 5th grade, and along your life on this Earth, please include failures in it. Thanks, my Queen." Theresa explained with a trembling voice.

"I have heard you," replied Crystal and disappeared.

Crystal understood what Theresa meant. She, however, had a reputation to maintain now. Thus, she excelled in third grade but then decided to fail the fifth grade.

After school, Crystal took farming training from her grandmother. Crystal eagerly followed her grandmother through the lush green fields, her eyes wide with wonder as she watched the older woman expertly plant rows of bananas, cassavas, yams, maize, peanuts, and tomatoes. She watched in awe as her grandmother carefully tended to each plant, nurturing them with love and care.

As the seasons changed, Crystal learned the secrets of the land, how to read the signs of the weather, and how to coax the best from each crop. Her grandmother's wisdom and knowledge were like a treasure trove, and Crystal knew she would always carry them with her.

Theresa had a cocoa and coffee farm and showed everything about it to Crystal. She even showed her medicinal plants. One day, she went far away with Crystal alone and showed her the most powerful plants that can heal almost everything.

"It is the Palmyra that can eradicate cancer cells." She had said.

Crystal had always been a curious child, eager to explore the world around her. As she grew into a young woman, her beauty only added to her allure. But she knew that her true test was yet to come. She had always sensed that there was something more to life than what she had experienced so far. And as she looked out at the world around her, she knew that she was right.

At the tender age of 23, she found herself standing at the altar, ready to marry the man she had been destined to be with since birth. Beelzebub, the dark and mysterious figure who had captured her heart, stood before her, his piercing gaze sending shivers down her spine. He took a human body to be able to marry Crystal, and they got transferred to another country. As they exchanged vows, she couldn't help but wonder what her future would hold.

A few months after they arrived in the country, Crystal noticed that she was followed. No matter where she went, she could feel eyes on her. It was as if she had a group of followers who were always lurking in the shadows, waiting for her next move. She even saw a camera in front of her master bedroom window. They moved then to another house. She even received a visit from the country's National Guard one day.

“Is your husband home?” he asked, eyeing her suspiciously.

She hesitated for a moment, wondering why he needed to know. But then she remembered the recent break-ins and realized he was just doing his job.

“No, he's out of town,” she replied, trying to sound confident.

But no matter how much security pulled up at her home, she never felt safe. Oftentimes, the silence in the apartment building was broken by the sound of muffled voices. It was a common occurrence, as the walls were thin and the soundproofing was inadequate. Her neighbors hurled insults and called her names like “witch” and "imbecile."

With time, the voices only grew louder and more threatening.

"We will launch Interpol," They said, "We will follow you everywhere. We will put cameras even in your village."

"You give birth to monsters," They spat. "We will never allow you to have children again."

She often had to bear insults about her Father, Olian too. But Crystal couldn’t help herself. Instead, she would sit alone in her room, her thoughts consumed by the words that had been spoken to her. They had threatened her and warned her not to have any more children. She couldn't shake the fear that had taken hold of her since that day. Every time she thought about the possibility of bringing another life into the world, she was filled with dread. She didn't know how they could possibly make good on their threat, but the fear was real.

Chapter 9

Crystal knew that her powers were a gift, and she couldn't resist them anymore, especially when she was faced with a choice between life and death. No matter what the cost, she was determined to fulfill her purpose. She didn't know what the future held, but she knew that she was put on this Earth for a reason.

One day, while walking down the street, she saw a woman fall to the ground. The woman seemed to have lost consciousness. Crystal knew that she had to act fast.

Soon a crowd formed around the women. Crystal stood there for a split second, questioning if she should intervene. Before a second could pass, Crystal was beside the woman.

She asked the crowd to let her pray for the woman, and they obliged. Crystal placed her hand on the woman's forehead and began to pray. Suddenly, the woman came to and sat up, looking around in confusion. The crowd was amazed. They had witnessed a miracle.

The director couldn't believe what he had heard the day before. Yet, everyone was talking about how Crystal had saved the woman. As the person in authority, he felt like he had to acknowledge the assistance.

“We want to thank you for what you did yesterday,” he emphasized. “You saved the life of this student, and we don’t know how to thank you.”

Crystal replied humbly, “Don’t thank me, but thank God.”

From that day on, Crystal started using her powers to help others whenever she could. One day, as she was walking home, it started raining heavily. Crystal saw as the rain began to flood and destroy the fields, so she simply commanded the rain to stop. And it did!

She would often control the sun's movements. She would raise the sun when it was too dark outside and would make it set when she wanted.

Crystal knew that with great power came great responsibility, and she made sure no one suspected anything. She couldn’t help but run into one problem after the other, and she knew she was supposed to put on this Earth to solve these problems. She was determined to use her gifts for good.

One day, Crystal decided to darken the entire neighborhood by shutting down all the lights. The electricians were called to fix the problem, but they were unable to find a solution. Despite their best efforts, the lights remained off throughout the day. As the sun began to set, the residents of the neighborhood grew increasingly worried about the prolonged outage.

One of the electricians suggested that they give up, as they had never encountered such a problem before. Another electrician, however, thought that they should try a different approach. He believed that the problem might be more spiritual than physical and suggested that they pray to the ghosts of the land for assistance. The other electricians were skeptical, but they had nothing to lose, so they left the case unresolved and went home.

Meanwhile, the residents of the neighborhood continued to grumble about the darkness, unaware of the danger that was approaching. Unbeknownst to them, a storm was brewing, and it was heading straight for their village. If the storm made contact with the electricity wires, it would cause massive destruction.

However, the goddess Crystal had foreseen the coming storm and had intentionally shut down the lights to protect the village. As the storm raged on, the electricity wires remained untouched, and the village was spared from disaster.

The next day, the electricians returned to the neighborhood to find that the lights had mysteriously been turned back on. They were confused and bewildered, unable to explain how the problem had been resolved. The Goddess Crystal had saved them from the storm, and they were grateful for her intervention.

In the spiritual world, whenever anyone needed help, they would call out Crystal's name, and she would always be there to assist them. Crystal had the ability to enter the spiritual world and resolve any kind of problem. Her method was unique and effective. Whenever she needed to address an issue, she would call for a meeting with all the spirits of the universe and send them to work on her behalf. These spirits would go all over the world to resolve any issues they encountered. Once they completed their tasks, they would return to Crystal with their results.

Sometimes, when she called for a meeting, she would invite all the spirits of the universe, including animals, gods, and goddesses, to decide what to do. During meetings, everyone would offer suggestions on how to resolve issues, but the final decision was hers. She even had the power to choose who would run for president and sent spirits to every country to make it happen.

However, there were specific spirits that worked to accomplish her requests. She prayed to Yahweh to intervene in the name of Jesus, and these spirits would follow her commands. With her exceptional ability, Crystal was able to help people all over the world.

Crystal assisted doctors by advising them on how to handle complicated cases, helping physicians discover new medications, and providing food and money to people in need. She assisted many organizations and granted their requests. Her powers were so vast that she even called for rain for farmers and ordered the sea to be calmer. She was able to help scientists discover new things and find new ways to learn and explain their discoveries. She was instrumental in building everything in the world, from buildings to bridges.

Crystal was also a talented musician. She often played her musical instruments, especially the Kora, an African guitar. This helped her resolve the world's problems. One day, while playing the Kora in her living room, she called upon all the spirits of the universe to work on her behalf and answer her questions. They provided her with guidance on how to help others.

Crystal faced many problems on her own and often found herself thinking out loud,

“I miss Minet.”

Her beloved cat had disappeared into the forest when Olian passed away. Unbeknownst to Crystal, Harlan was always by her side, even if she couldn't feel his presence. At that moment, he was like the wind, surrounding her. Despite this, Crystal felt as though she was all alone on Earth without him.

Chapter 10

The council meeting was a grand and formal affair, with all the most influential individuals in attendance. Presidents from around the world, deities from the globe, and other powerful figures had all gathered together to discuss an important matter: Crystal's nomination to become the president of all presidents in the world.

The atmosphere was tense but also electric with anticipation. Everyone knew that this was a momentous occasion that could shape the future of the world. The room was filled with a sense of excitement and awe as the attendees took their seats at the table.

The chairs were ornate and made of the finest materials, each one designed to reflect the personality and power of its occupant. The walls were adorned with intricate designs and artwork depicting scenes of power and majesty.

They were all in search of someone who could lead the world to greater heights and bring peace and prosperity to every corner of the globe. Crystal was the perfect candidate for the position, but there was one problem. Her identity had to remain a secret. Everyone knew that if her true identity was revealed, it could jeopardize her chances of becoming the president. They needed someone to guide her without her knowing it.

The Earth Goddess suggested that they turn to Harlan, the most powerful hypnotist in the spiritual world. Harlan was known for his ability to hypnotize anyone without them realizing it. He could guide Crystal without her ever knowing it. The council agreed with the suggestion, and they summoned Harlan to the council meeting. Harlan was intrigued by the proposal and agreed to help.

Harlan announced, “I have heard you. What we should do is hypnotize her in her physical body. That’s all.”

“How will it work, oh, powerful God?” Someone asked.

Harlan already knew what he was going to do. He would hypnotize Crystal and guide her through everything, from her daily routine to her decision-making process. He would be her doctor, nurse, gym coach, dietitian, and principal advisor.

Harlan told him, “I will hypnotize her myself and tell her what she has to do in everything so that her real identity will remain secret. There will be secret guards all around her for her physical and spiritual protection.”

“How would you do that, my Highness?”

“It’s a secret for now,” replied Harlan. “We should start the process as soon as possible. I will come every night to visit her with my physical body, but she won’t be aware of it until one day, she will start knowing everything in her human body. I will be her everything. So, let’s start the process now.”

The process began on a dark and stormy night when Harlan visited Crystal. He hypnotized her, and in a trance-like state, Crystal received instructions on how to become the president of all presidents on Earth. Harlan's hypnotic suggestions were powerful and effective, and the process was a success. The next morning, Harlan left Crystal to awaken on her own, and when she did, she was filled with a newfound sense of purpose.

As the newly appointed president of all presidents, Crystal had a lot on her plate. She was responsible for advising leaders worldwide, and before they made any big decisions, they sought her permission and guidance. Crystal was determined to make the world a better place, and she tackled every issue with poise and grace.

She dealt with everything that came her way, from finding solutions to global issues to saving lives and even giving birth to new ideas. Her incredible leadership skills were recognized by even her greatest adversaries, like Beelzebub, who surrendered to her and began to transform into a more benevolent entity before the eyes of the world. Crystal's presidency was a turning point for humanity, and her legacy will be remembered for generations to come.

It reminded her of an encounter she had with a strange man when she was only seventeen years old. Crystal vividly remembered the incident from her time at boarding school. As she was walking to class, a man passing by wished her good luck. Intrigued, Crystal turned to greet the man and asked him why he was wishing her good luck. The man replied, saying that he could tell that Crystal was someone who believed that good would ultimately triumph over evil.

The encounter always put a smile on Crystal's face. It served for her as a reminder of how far she had come. There was once a time when Earth was filled with nothing but hate, poverty, and disease. Yet, Crystal had made these issues disappear from the face of Earth.

The Earth King was extremely grateful to Crystal and to everyone who helped find a solution to the world's problems. The people of Earth began to improve, and things they had always wanted in their lives became available. New medications were discovered, and everything began to return to normal. The flowers started to glow, and greenery appeared everywhere, making the Earth a beautiful planet. Animals became happy and started to become friends with one another. The prisoners were freed, and there were no more robberies, murders, or enemies; freedom was everywhere.

The world was finally at peace, and the people of Earth were overjoyed. A riot started shouting,

"Freedom has come, freedom has come, freedom has come at last!"

The people were ecstatic and celebrated their newfound freedom. They praised Crystal and all the gods and goddesses who had helped to make this possible.

Crystal and Harlan decided to stay on Earth and decided to renew their vows. The ceremony was breathtaking, and everyone was in awe. It was a peaceful day, and birds chirped in the background. Surrounding the couple were the goddesses and gods, all dressed in their finest clothes. It was a magnificent sight to see. Crystal and Harlan stood together, gazing into each other's eyes with pure love and devotion. Everyone watched with reverence as the couple promised their love and devotion to each other

The couple started their life together on Earth. They still visited Venus once in a while to see their Father.

Beelzebub, who had once been a demon, became a good spirit. He took a human body again and married a beautiful lady. He was no longer the evil entity he once was. All of Crystal's trials stopped, and she ruled the universe from Earth. The world had never been happier, and it was all thanks to Crystal and her powers.

Printed by Libri Plureos GmbH in Hamburg,
Germany